I'm a Big Sister

Goldest Karat Publishing
400 West Peachtree Street
Suite #4-513
Atlanta, GA 30308

For more books, visit us online at
www.goldestkarat.com

This book is dedicated to my niece Olivia and every other little girl who has just become a big sister.

Mommy and Daddy were gone for a while
Then they came back home with a great big smile

Wrapped up in a blanket held by my mother
Was my brand new, tiny, baby brother!

Daddy showed me baby's bib

His clothes, his toys and baby's crib

And tiny hats for baby's head

Baby's feet are too tiny to walk

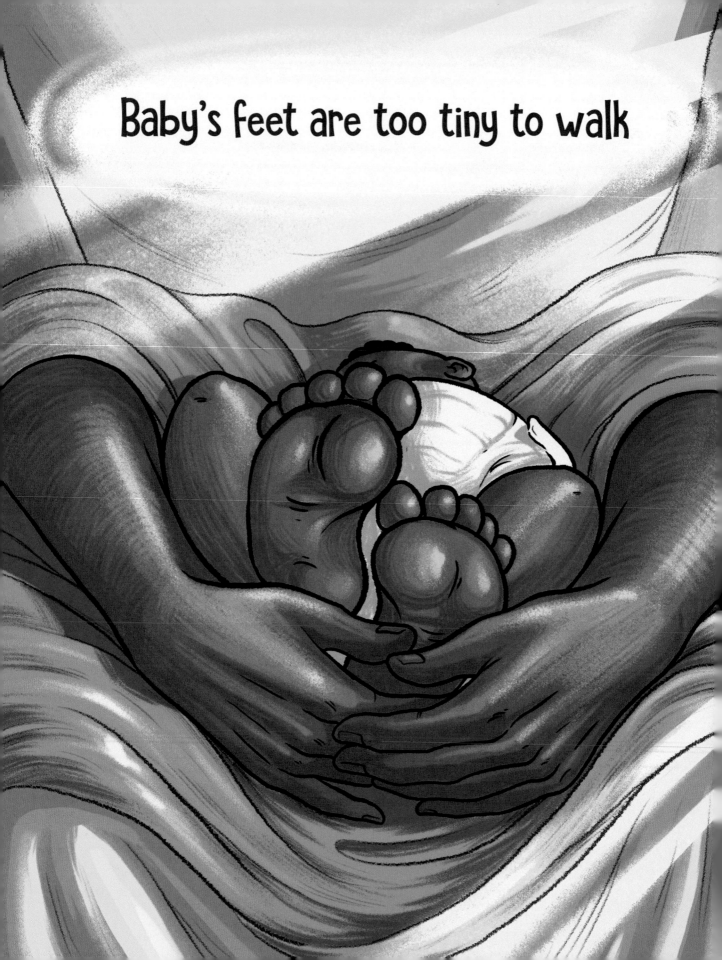

And baby doesn't know how to talk

But if baby feels like something's wrong
His cry is loud and long and strong!

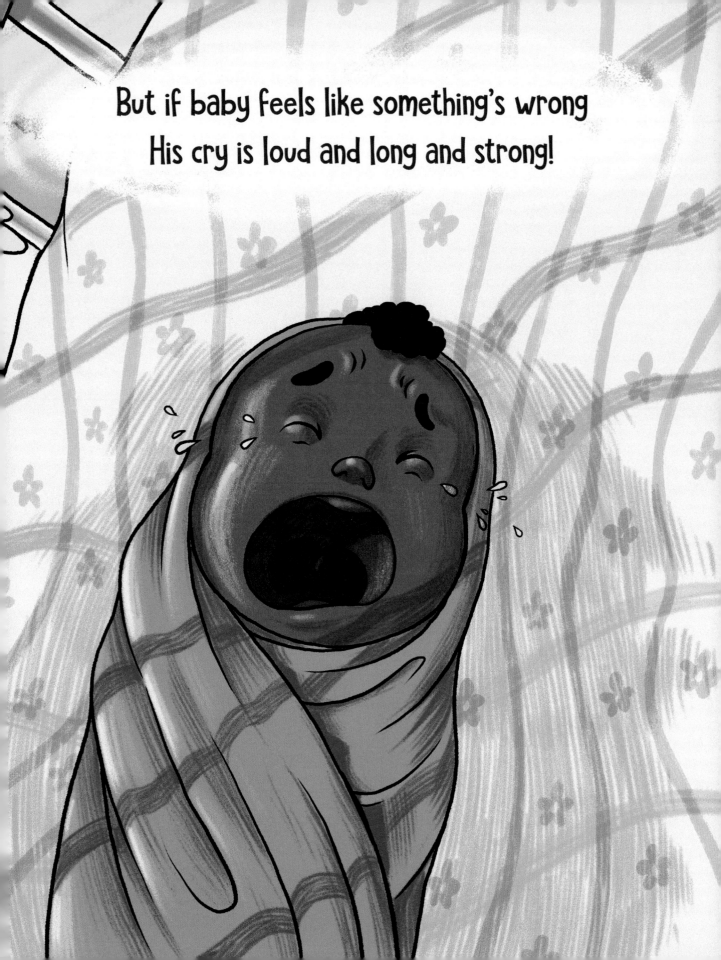

Baby is short and I am tall

But baby can grab onto things
Like fingers, blankets, hair, and strings

Baby loves baths in his tiny tub

I play with my duck
And sing Rub-a-dub-dub

Then on my tippy toes I creep
To make sure baby stays asleep

Mommy told me she can see
What a good sister I will be

After she kisses me goodnight,
mom tucks me in to bed real tight

I'm so glad baby is here
I'll be big sister of the year

Even though life with a baby is new
I love being a big sister and so will you!

For Andrea.
I wish you nothing
but the best!!

Thanks for the support

Klein

Made in the USA
Coppell, TX
03 March 2020

For Fatima and Mariam

I hope this book whets your appetite for your first trip to Naija.

The Amazing Road Trip in Nigeria

Akin Durosimi

Sade and her younger brother, Wale are about to go on a road trip with their dad, Mr. Johnson. They were going to visit exciting places all over Nigeria.

Their first destination was to Olumo rock. The Olumo rock is a popular tourist attraction used as a fortress many years ago. It is in the city of Abeokuta, which is the state capital of Ogun state. Abeokuta means "Under the rock."

There was an elevator you could ride all the way to the top.

However, Sade wanted to do something more challenging. "Daddy, can we take the stairs instead?"

Mr. Johnson smiled and replied, "If you guys are up for the exercise, we can take the stairs to the top."

Once they reached the top of the rock, they saw a stunning view of the entire city. The roofs of all the houses and buildings created an endless sea of brown. It was very pretty indeed.

"Daddy, now where are we going?" Wale asked eagerly.
"To see the National Arts Theater! It's a wonderful place to watch plays and concerts or have a picnic."
"Cool! Where is it located?" Sade asked.
"It is located in Lagos."
So, they got on the Lagos-Abeokuta expressway and drove towards their next destination.

Sade was fascinated by the shape of the National Arts Theater.

She asked, "Why does the shape of the theater look so different from other buildings?"

Mr. Johnson explained, "The design of the building is based off another building called the Palace of Culture and Sports in Bulgaria which is shaped like a soldier's hat."

Mr. Johnson said, "There is a stage play about a Queen named Moremi. Would you guys like to watch it?"
"Yes!" exclaimed the two children in unison.
It was so much fun to watch the play, and the children were very happy to learn about the brave queen.

After watching the play, Mr. Johnson took the kids to eat. The food was very yummy and the children couldn't stop talking about the play.

The next day, Mr. Johnson got the kids up early so they could continue their road trip. "Kids, it is time for us to head to the beach! I know Wale loves building sand castles."

"Me too!" said Sade.

"Fine!" said Mr. Johnson, "Then let's head to the longest sand beach in West Africa!"

"What is the name of this beach?" Sade asked as the car got back onto the highway.
"It's called Ibeno beach and it's located in Akwa Ibom state," replied her dad.

Once they got to the beach, the children raced towards the water. Mr. Johnson followed closely behind.

They joined the beachgoers and tossed the ball around. The sun was hot, which made the soft breeze and the cool water feel good on the skin.

The children's next destination was the Thought Pyramid Art Center in Abuja.
Mr. Johnson said, "The Thought Pyramid Art Center has a lot of wonderful art exhibitions and also offers art classes for children."

The children learned there was also an Arts Library that helps in research of modern African & Nigerian art. As they walked through the huge building, they admired the beautiful paintings and sculptures.

After a long drive, Mr. Johnson suggested stopping to buy suya from a roadside vendor. The children loved suya, which is thinly sliced grilled meat. A very popular snack all over Nigeria.

The next day, they got on the road early again.
"Kids, would you like to see some wild animals in their
natural habitat?" Mr. Johnson asked.
They both replied, "Yes, Daddy!"
"Okay, let's drive to the Yankari National Park in Bauchi
state."
They drove towards Bauchi in northeastern Nigeria.

Once they got to the park they boarded a safari jeep. As they drove along, Sade yelled, "There's an elephant!" Then Wale pointed towards a baboon.

They stopped to have a picnic by a lovely warm water spring. The children learned there were actually several warm water springs in the park.

After the picnic, the children were very sleepy since was late in the evening. So, Mr. Johnson headed towards a hotel for a good night's rest. Tomorrow, they would all wake up refreshed for the long journey back home.

Wale fell asleep as soon as his head hit the pillow. Sade could not stop talking about the road trip. She was filled with a sense of pride and was happy she got to visit so many beautiful places. She wondered when she would get to explore more states in her amazing country: Nigeria.

Made in the USA
Coppell, TX
03 March 2020